The Magic Dragons of Anglesey

Book One

by

Conrad Jones

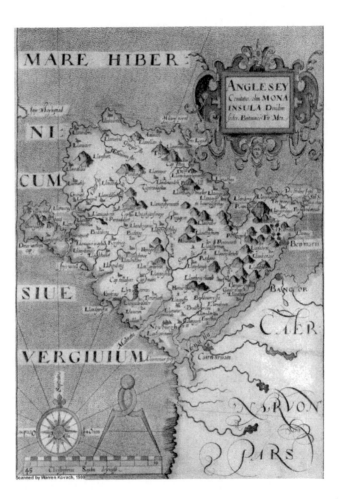

MARE HIBER

ANGLESEY
Comitatus, olim MONA
INSULA Druidibus
sedes. Britannicè Tir Môn.

NI

CUM

SIUE

VERGIUIUM

CAER

Beavmaris

BANGOR

NARVON

PARS

Christopherus Saxton describsit

The Ancient Stones of Anglesey

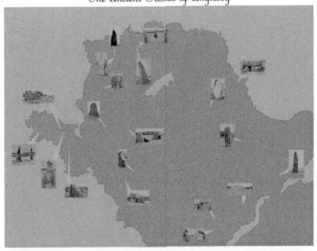

The Magic
Dragons of Anglesey

A Dragon Cave at Holyhead Mountain

HEN GOCH (OLD RED)

CHAPTER 1

Once upon a time, not too long ago, in a

land at the very edge of Wales, there was

an island which was as old as time itself

and time is very old.

Two-hundred years ago, you would

have to travel there by boat as the Menai

Bridge wasn't built until 1826. Now, there

are two bridges linking the mainland to

the island and they were built by the

humans.

CONRAD JONES

Humans are very good at building things. In fact, I bet your house was built by humans.

At the furthest point of the island is yet another one, called Holy Island, and you have to cross the inland sea to get there. Of course, you can cross by road nowadays, but that wasn't always the case.

Towering above Holy Island is a mysterious mountain often hidden in clouds and dragon smoke; it's mostly made from limestone and beyond the mountain is nothing but the sea as far

2

you can see. Humans have lived on the
mountain since the Iron Age, which was a
very long time ago. About six thousand
years ago in fact.

What most people don't realise is that
beneath the mountain, in a deep dark
cave, Hen Goch the dragon lived. She was
the oldest and biggest dragon of all.

There used to be a pub at the bottom
of the mountain in a place called
Llaingoch, which was named after her,
but it's gone now. She was similar to the
dragon on the Welsh flag, but much
bigger and far more frightening. The

3

dragon was called Old Red, but she was only red when she was angry. The rest of the time she was grey, like the ancient rocks which surrounded her, and that made her very difficult to see unless she moved or opened one of her huge eyes.

She hadn't always lived in Holyhead Mountain, Old Red used to live in a cavern beneath Mount Snowden before humans began climbing it in their thousands. Snowdonia was once remote and difficult to access but the humans built roads and hotels and then to top it all, they built a railway track and put a steam train on it.

THE MAGIC DRAGONS OF ANGLESEY

Can you imagine the noise of a train going

up down above your cave when you're

having a dragon nap?

In the summer months, the humans

were like ants swarming all over the

mountain in their big boots, stomping up

and stomping back down. Red couldn't

sleep with all the noise and dragons need

lots of sleep, so she found a smaller

mountain at Holyhead next to the sea

where the humans couldn't stomp around

all over it. Because of the sea, one side

would always be off limits as humans

can't walk on water. Not all of them,

anyway.

'Oh, I'm so tired,' said Old Red,

waking up after a ten-year nap. She

opened one eye lazily and then closed it

again. It was night time and the world

outside was dark.

'I might just have another sleep,' she

said, turning over but a noise from the

distance bothered her. 'Something woke

me up before I'm ready and I wonder

what it was?'

Old Red knew that she couldn't just go

back to sleep without checking around

the mountain to see what it was that had

awoken her. Dragons are curious

creatures and need to know everything

about everything. She opened her eyes

and yawned, and dark blue smoke poured

from her nostrils like soot from a

chimney. Her old joints were stiff and

creaky and full of arthritis because she

was, after all, two million years old.

She stretched her huge back and the

scales on her skin rubbed and clicked and

groaned as they rubbed against each

other. Sparks sprayed into the air as she

made her way slowly but surely towards
the opening of her cave.

It was night-time and she could see
the beam of light coming from South
Stack Lighthouse. It was to her left and
the beam of light made its way across the
sea as far as she could see, which was
almost to the Emerald Isle, or that's what
they used to call it.

Leprechauns and unicorns used to live
there, but the humans went to war with
each other and all the peaceful creatures
left. You will never find a unicorn or
leprechauns anywhere near a war.

Negative situations make them ill and so they move far away from them. Old Red knew all the unicorns back in the old days, but now she only saw them once in a blue moon, which wasn't very often. There were none on Anglesey anymore either.

She knew the woodland fairies were still there, but they were skilled at hiding and keeping themselves concealed. And the water nymphs were still there, too. Rumour had it that a lot of nymphs were active on the island, but they kept themselves to themselves and were

always busy nymphing about.

There were a few elves about too,

Penrhos had a community of them and

Newborough Forest hosted several. She

made a note to look them all up and

make sure everything was as it should be.

The wind picked up and whistled through

her cave, disturbing her thoughts.

The wind was howling that night and

the rain was lashing down, the drops

turning to steam as they landed on her

skin. The waves were crashing against

Holyhead Mountain and they made a huge

swooshing sound almost like thunder.

Red listened as only dragons can, their

hearing is incredibly powerful but then

everything about a dragon is powerful,

especially the females. From the distance,

Red heard men calling for help and she

could hear the fear in their voices. A boat

was in peril somewhere out there in the

darkness. The voices were drifting on the

wind, which was distorting the sound and

making it difficult to pinpoint exactly

where they were. She listened again for a

short time, and she knew that the voices

were coming from the open sea beyond

the Skerries Lighthouse. There were human sailors in peril out there and there was only one thing to do, which was to help them.

Now, you have to remember that Red is the biggest dragon and being the biggest dragon ever, makes it very difficult to leave your cave and be unseen and of course being unseen is a very important part of being a dragon. With a shimmy of her scales, they became mirror-like and made her almost invisible. She was very skilled at moving about without the humans seeing her.

She listened once again and then called out. Her voice sounded like a foghorn, deep and booming. Sometimes, if you listen carefully, you can hear Red calling from beneath the mountain. When she calls, her breath makes a steamy mist, which hangs above the summit.

Red called again and she saw the sea beginning to foam, near the mouth of her cave. The head and shoulders of a mermaid appeared from the waves. She was joined by several others, drawn by her call for help.

'Grace, you look as beautiful as ever,' Red said, puffing smoke from her nostrils. Of course, dragons are very charming indeed. 'Thank you all for coming.'

'Hen Goch. It's so good to see you,' she said. 'We heard you call for help.'

'Yes. I can hear a boat in distress, somewhere beyond the Skerries,' Red said. Grace looked confused and shook her head. 'What is it?' Red asked.

'We can't interfere in the matters of men anymore,' Grace said. 'The humans have long since given up caring for the

14

planet. They no longer care for

themselves or each other.'

'When did pity and compassion apply

to what race or species we are?' the old

dragon asked, shaking her head.

'Until the humans discover pity and

compassion for each other, Mother Earth

has said we must leave them to their own

end,' Grace said. 'I'm sorry, Red, but we

can't interfere. Their fate is in their own

hands.' She blew a kiss. 'Farewell, my old

friend. You take care of yourself.'

And with that kiss, she was gone

beneath the waves in a plume of bubbles.

Red shook her head sadly. She took a

deep breath and steam poured from her

ears. She held her breath and dived

beneath the waves. You may not know

that dragons are just as at home

underwater as they are above it, but they

are, and can stay beneath the waves for

hours and hours.

Anyway, I'm digressing. Red swam

faster than a torpedo, and she was soon

beneath the crippled fishing boat. The

propellors weren't turning and she

couldn't hear the engine. Without an

engine, the boat was being tossed around

like a twig in a washing machine. As she

swam towards the surface, she could see

the whole boat was being tossed and torn by the wind and the waves. Red knew that the sailors didn't have very long unless she did something to help them.

Red swam beneath the boat and came up within a few feet of the surface, feeling the vessel settle between the ears on the top of her head.

Gently, she turned and headed back towards the port of Holyhead, where the breakwater would shelter them. The men on the boat were shocked into silence. They realised that something was driving them from beneath the waves, but they didn't have a clue it was Old Red the

dragon saving their lives and taking them

back to the port.

Within an hour or so, Old Red had

pushed the boat around the breakwater

into the relative safety of the harbour,

where the coast guards were launching to

help the hapless fishermen.

Once Red knew the men were safe,

she dived deep, almost touching the

seabed with her scaly talons. Red used

her huge wings beneath the water, which

propelled her at a frightening speed back

towards her cave.

She reached the cave and climbed out of the deep water into the shallows and then onto the rocks and the safety of her cavernous home. The seawater was dripping from her wings and her scales forming puddles on the rocks, the sound echoing deep into the mountain.

Red breathed out and fire exploded from her mouth, heating the rocks and making all the water evaporate.

Within seconds, she was dry.

Anglesey and Snowdonia where Old Red used to live

Chapter 2

Red sensed the presence of another dragon immediately. She snorted fire from her nostrils to illuminate the farther reaches of the cave and sure enough, snoozing in the darkness was Glas Bach, or Little Blue as he was known. Little Blue was a much smaller but just as sleepy dragon. He liked to nod off wherever he could.

Red had not seen Little Blue for at least five years as they both enjoyed a

22

nap but woke up at different times, so
when Blue slept, Red was awake and
when Red slept, Blue had been awake.
Little Blue is quite small for a dragon, not
much taller than a man, but much
heavier, as dragons are made of very
dense stuff.

Because he is much smaller than
most other dragons, Little Blue liked to
climb, so he can see for miles. Blue was a
very nosey dragon and liked to keep an
eye on what was going on. He was also
gifted with the ability to change colour
and blend into his surroundings, like his
distant cousins, the chameleons.

Of course, all lizards are descended from the smaller dragons who lived in China. I'm sure you've seen a Chinese dragon, like on the menu of your takeaway or on the television?

Forgive me, I'm waffling again.

Blue climbs things as high as he can, so he can see all around him and that makes him feel safe.

Little Blue and the other blue dragons look after the people on Anglesey, even the naughty ones. So, if that's where you are, you're very lucky to have a dragon looking out for you. Blue also has red eyes and I'll tell you a secret about where

24

THE MAGICAL DRAGONS OF ANGLESEY

he climbs sometimes, but don't tell
everyone. Blue climbs to the top of the
huge chimney at the Tinto factory
because he can see all the way across the
island to the mountains.

Of course, you know that the factory
hasn't been making anything for many
years and so the chimney is cold now but
sometimes, at night, Little Blue will climb
up to the top, wrap his long blue tail
around the chimney, and from there he
can look all over the sea and all over the
mountain and all over the island and
Snowdonia beyond.

Sometimes, if you're really lucky and you look at the chimney at night-time, you might see one of his red eyes glowing in the dark, but don't tell anybody else because where dragons climb is a secret. Anyway, on with the story.

'Hello, Little Blue,' said Old Red. 'I haven't seen you for a very long time and I've just woke up from a little nap. What brings you here?'

'I heard you calling and at first, I thought it was the foghorn at North Stack, but I would recognise that call anywhere. I'm glad you're awake because I needed to talk to you, as there's trouble on the

island,' said Little Blue.

'I knew there was something wrong

when I woke up,' said Old Red. 'I could

feel it in my bones.'

'I was going to wake you up years ago,

but I thought it would sort itself out.

Unfortunately, it hasn't,' said Little Blue.

'In my experience, things rarely sort

themselves out. In fact, things usually get

worse if you bury your head in the sand.

What did you think was going to sort itself

out?' Old Red asked.

'It all started with someone, or

something, stealing the milk from the

cows,' said Little Blue. 'And now they are stealing all the wool from the sheep.'

'Goodness gracious me,' said Old Red. 'Who on Earth would be stealing milk from the cows and wool from the sheep?'

'The same person who's stealing all the eggs from the hens,' Little Blue said. 'That's who.'

'They're stealing all the eggs from the hens as well?' Old Red asked, astounded by the news. 'It sounds to me like we've got a thief on the island. And a greedy thief, too.'

'We most certainly do,' said Little Blue, nodding. 'And I've been waiting for you to wake up to tell you what's going

on.'

'You should have come and woke me

up,' Old Red said.

'I know how grumpy you are when

you're woken up.'

'I am very grumpy when I'm tired. All

the same, you should have.'

'But you get grumpy.'

'Yes. I know.'

'And I don't like you when you're

grumpy.'

'Okay,' Old Red said. 'We have

established that I'm grumpy when I'm

tired. Now, tell me about the farmers.'

29

'They are very unhappy. They have got no food and no money and some of them have even left their farms and gone to England.'

'England? Surely, things can't be that bad,' Old Red said. 'That nasty man George was from England.'

'He slayed a dragon,' Little Blue said.

'Yes. I know,' Red said, frowning. 'That's why I called him nasty.' Smoke poured from her nostrils. 'George the dragon slayer, indeed. The dragon he killed was no more than a big lizard. The man told fibs, and everyone believed him.'

'Humans do that,' Little Blue said.

'The one in charge of England now tells

fibs.'

'Is that the human with the scruffy

head? Is he really still in charge of

England?'

'Yes. But the people there aren't

happy,' Blue explained. 'When the

humans had to lockdown, he was having

parties at his house when everyone else

had to stay at home and couldn't see

their families.'

'Ah well, that's humans for you.

Unfortunately, some of them think they're

better than others. This is their downfall.

31

They're not kind to each other.' Old Red

shook her head. 'We can't have our

farmers going to England. There is no

farmland for them in England. It's all been

sold. What are they going to do for a

living in England?'

'This is the problem, you see,' said

Little Blue. 'But all the markets had to

shut down. When it's time to milk the

cows and sell the milk, all the milk has

already gone. And the same thing

happened when it was time to shear the

sheep and sell wool for people to make

jumpers to sell at the Pringle mill. All the

wool was gone. The sheep were as bald as

a coot, freezing cold and not a ball of

wool to show for it.'

'Good heavens! Are you telling me

there are no jumpers in the Pringle mill?'

Red said, shocked.

'Nope. Not even the scratchy ones.

And it's even worse than that.'

'How can it be any worse?'

'Not only are there no jumpers, but

there are also no boxes of fudge for the

tourists to take back on the coaches to

Llandudno.'

'Shiver my timbers,' Red said,

shocked. 'No fudge. They will stop

coming to the place with the long name,'

Red said.

'Llanfairpwllgwyngyllgogerychwyrndro
bwlllantysiliogogogoch,' Little Blue said.

'No one likes a show-off,' Red said.

'Yes. That place.'

'Things have gone from bad to worse
and even the little chip shop across the
road from the mill has had to close its
doors.'

'This is a terrible situation. I don't
know why you didn't wake me up years
ago.'

'I know how grumpy you are when you
wake up,' Blue said.

'Yes. You've already pointed that out.'

'Sorry.' Old Red looked grumpy and thoughtful. 'What are you thinking?' Blue asked.

'I remember a time, thousands of years ago, when something similar happened to all the milk and all the eggs. Every morning, the farmers found their stock stolen. It took us years to realise one of the rock goblins had woken up and was pilfering everything it could from the farms at night-time.'

'Good heavens,' Little Blue said, shocked. 'A rock goblin?'

'Yes, a rock goblin,' Old Red said.

'And there are two of the most famous rock goblins of all time on Holy Island.'

'I know one on the Porth Dafarch road,' Blue said, thinking. 'The Carreg y Bwgan.'

'Yes. He was a particularly naughty rock goblin,' Red said, thinking. 'Is he still there?'

'Yes,' Blue said, nodding. 'I saw him last night from the chimney. He hasn't moved for centuries.'

'Good. The other one is sitting on the beach at Porth-y-Post.' Old Red shrugged and her scales sparked. 'He's been sitting there for as long as I can remember.'

'What happened to him?'

'He was stealing milk and eggs and not just the wool, but the entire sheep,' Red explained. 'He was a greedy goblin. The wizard from the tin mines at Parys Mountain turned him to stone for a million years. Of course, one day the spell will wear off and the greedy little goblin will be up to her old tricks again.' Old Red shook her head and yawned, and a plume of orange flame exploded from her nostrils nearly burning Little Blue, who had to jump out of the way.

37

'Goodness me, you clumsy old dragon,' Little Blue said. 'You nearly burnt my bottom.'

'Burning your bottom is the least of our troubles,' Old Red said. 'We need to put a stop to this tomfoolery and mischief before there are no farmers left on the island and the Pringle mill closes down.'

'And how do you propose we do that?' Little Blue asked.

'We must call a meeting of the Wizards and Dragons at the standing stones at Ty Mawr,' Old Red said.

'All of them?'

'Yes. All of them. No excuses.'

'What about the mermaids?' Blue asked. 'They can't get there.'

'No. Sadly, they have decided that the fate of men is in their own hands.'

'What about the witches?' Little blue asked.

'The problem with the witches is most of them are related to the goblins and nymphs,' Old Red explained. 'And it will be a full moon. I think it's probably best not to tell them just yet. We can tell them at the last minute and then they can decide if they're in the right frame of mind to come without causing an argument.'

'I agree. We don't want to get on the wrong side of the witches,' Little Blue said. 'You know how touchy they can be especially at the full moon. They can be so moody and there is no talking to them when they are in that kind of mood. And the Nymphs?'

'They're always busy nymphing about,' Red said, shaking her head. 'We can invite them, but I don't think they can help at this stage.'

'What about the green dragons?' Blue asked.

'What about them?' Red asked.

'They've fallen out with the yellows,'

Blue explained.

'Why?'

'Because they're yellow and not

green,' Blue said.

'I've never heard anything so

ridiculous in all my centuries on Earth. I

have never heard of a dragon taking issue

with another dragon because of the colour

of their scales,' Red said. 'You tell the

greens and the yellows that unless I've

missed something, we're all dragons and

they will behave like dragons with dignity

and respect for each other, or they will be

explaining themselves to me.' Red was

angry and she snorted. Two plumes of fire

exploded from her nostrils and Blue had

to jump out of the way once again.

'I told them you wouldn't be happy,'

Blue said.

'And what did they say?'

'They said you wouldn't understand as

you're a grey,' Blue said.

'They're all descended from one

bloodline. My bloodline,' Red roared, and

her voice boomed in the cavern. 'We all

came from the greys. I won't tolerate

such nonsense,' Red said. 'We're

dragons, each and every one of us and I

won't hear any more of this ridiculous

42

nonsense.' Red shook her head and breathed fire. Blue jumped out of the way again. 'The humans have been discriminating against each other for centuries and look where it has got them. War and pestilence cover the planet.'

'Absolutely,' Blue said. 'Once we start favouring one colour over another, it's a slippery slope to trouble.'

'Indeed, it is. So, we are agreed then,' Old Red said. 'Let's set the meeting for midnight tomorrow.'

'I'll let everyone know to meet at the Ty Mawr stones,' Little Blue said. 'It's so good to see you again my old friend, and

I'm glad you're back with us.'

'It's good to see you too, Blue,' Old

Red said.

THE ROCK GOBLIN AT PORTH-Y-POST

HEAD   FACE

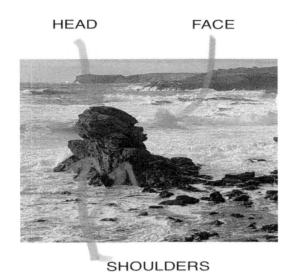

SHOULDERS

CHAPTER 3

Old Red didn't sleep at all that night, but then she had been asleep for a very long time and her thoughts were muddled by events on the island.

The thought of another rock goblin being on the loose was troubling her. You see, rock goblins are not very pleasant creatures. They are greedy, they are mysterious and monstrous, and they are trouble with a capital T. Rock goblins are so fast and are voracious eaters, never satisfied and always hungry and they decimate farmland and livestock. Some of the rock goblins Red had seen over the years were very big and very strong and very naughty. They often picked their noses and ate their bogeys, and they trumped all day long without excusing themselves.

The rock goblin at Carreg y Bwgan on Porth Dafarch Road was one of the worst she had ever encountered. It had taken all the magic the dragons could muster to turn him into a standing stone for a thousand years. Even the wizards hadn't been able to tame him. It was dragon magic which entombed him.

The local humans knew the rock as
Carreg y Bwgan, carreg meaning stone
and bwgan meaning ghost. So, the ghost
stone is actually a rock goblin, turned to
stone for being naughty and there were
lots of local myths and legends
surrounding it.

One of them was that if you run
around the stole three times backwards at
midnight, the ghost would jump out.
Another was that if you watched your
friends run around the stone three times,
it would open up and snatch them away
and they would never be seen again.
Some people said if you ran round, it

49

twelve times, you would see who you would marry. Of course, that was all nonsense. It was just a way of scaring little children into behaving themselves. Adults will say, if you don't behave, we'll take you to the Carreg y Bwgan, and let the bogeyman take you away. It was probably better that they didn't know the truth because rock goblins are far scarier than a bogeyman.

What Red needed to do was find out where this rock goblin was hiding during the daytime, if it was indeed a rock goblin stealing everything, and he couldn't be sure of that just yet. Red thought about what had happened since she been

awake.

It was always a pleasure to see Grace

and the other mermaids. They were so

pretty and such delightful creatures, but

it saddened her that they no longer

wanted to help the humans. After all,

someone had to help them because they

couldn't help themselves. They seem to

be destined to destroy themselves with

greed and vanity and money and all the

other silly things that humans treasured

instead of kindness and mercy. They were

the things which made the Earth turn and

the only things that would keep it turning

for generations to come. Kindness was in

short supply, sadly, and Red knew that if

the humans didn't start being nice to

each other, their species would decline.

THE CARREG-Y-BWGAN, PORTH DAFARCH RD

CHAPTER 4

Red didn't waste any time trying to sleep
and there was too much to do, anyway. She
took to the air and spread her huge wings,
taking off above the waves before circling
the mountain and heading off to
Snowdonia.

The island below her was in darkness
and from above, the streetlights twinkled
like yellow jewels against black velvet.
Behind her, in the northern sky, the green
glow of the aurora borealis touched the
horizon. It didn't take her long to reach

Tryfan and the entrance to the secret cave where some of the other greys lived.

There were six other greys in the Snowdonia Mountains and a sprinkling of yellows and a couple of greens further south towards Llangollen. They all lived there in relative peace and harmony, although Red wasn't sure how they put up with the constant noise of the humans marching up and down the mountains and the pesky steam train rattling along through the summer months.

Red used the secret entrance to the mountain, which was beneath the deep dark waters of Llyn Idwal, beneath the

Devil's Kitchen. She swam to the mouth of the cavern and called out her arrival. She heard a grumbling from deep below him and a short time later she saw the orange glow of a dragon approaching. It was Big Grey, the oldest and wisest dragon left in Snowdonia.

'Well, look who's here. If it isn't Old Red,' Grey said. 'It's about time you showed your scaly face around here. There's been all kinds of shenanigans going on while you've been asleep and it's time, we did something about it.'

'I've only just been made aware of what's going on.'

'What exactly is going on?' Grey asked, frowning.

'Livestock is being interfered with. We have a serial thief on the loose. The farmers on the island are leaving in droves. There is no milk in the supermarkets, no eggs in the shops, and there are no jumpers at the Pringle Mill.'

'No jumpers at the Pringle Mill?' Grey said. 'Not even the prickly ones?'

'None at all. It's a disaster,' Old Red said.

'I think we're sharing the same problem. We've had sheep and goats

going missing for nearly a year now,' Grey
said. 'The hill farmers are nearly broke.'

'I remember the same thing
happening a long time ago, do you?' Old
Red asked.

'I do. Are you talking about the rock
goblin at Carreg y Bwgan?' Grey asked.

'I am indeed talking about the rock
goblin. Nothing else makes sense. All the
eggs have been stolen from the hens
before the farmers even have chance to
wake up. And all the milk is being drunk
from the cows before the farmers have
chance to milk them. And all the sheep on
the island are bald, their wool taken

before the farmers can sheer them.' Red shook her head and her eyes darkened, and black smoke billowed from her nostrils.

'There isn't a creature anywhere with that kind of appetite and is fast enough to steal all the farmers' produce night after night week after week month after month. The only creature fast enough and voracious enough to do this is a rock goblin.'

'You could be right, but all the rock goblins were captured and entombed a long, long, time ago. None of those spells have run their course yet, so how can it

be a rock goblin?'

'The only way it can be another one, is

if one of them has been released from the

bowels of the earth accidentally,' Red

said.

'But how?' Grey asked. 'We keep an

eye on all the subterranean passageways

through the mountains.'

'I think the humans are probably

responsible without even knowing what

they've done,' Red said. 'They are greedy

and that is what has caused this

problem.'

'They are greedy, we all know that, but how on earth could they release a rock goblin?'

'By seeking out what they are always seeking out,' Red said, shaking her head. 'Gold, my friend. Gold and money are the root of all evils. Have they been mining in the mountains again?'

'Yes.' Grey gestured to the west with a shake of his head. 'Welsh gold is in favour. The Clogau mine has been reopened again and the humans are buying jewellery from there by the ton. They're digging there day and night.'

'If that's true then I think we have the answer to our problem,' Red said. 'They have dug too deep in their search for riches. And we all know what lives in the deepest reaches of these mountains,' Red said, her voice deep and thoughtful. 'The humans have released a rock goblin on themselves without knowing. And the only way to stop him is with dragon magic.'

'If we're all experiencing such thefts, can it possibly be the work of a single rock goblin?'

'That was what is troubling me and why I came to see you,' Red said. 'If the humans have opened a chasm, it's possible more than one of them passed

through into our world.'

'We must turn them to stone,' Grey

said.

'Or we can send them back to where

they came from.'

'And how do you propose we convince

a rock goblin to go back into the bowels

of the earth where there is little of any

flavour to eat, and the sun never shines?'

Grey asked. 'They're rampaging around

North Wales eating and drinking

everything they can get their hands on.

They must think all their birthdays have

come on the same day. I think they're

having so much fun they're never going to
stop unless we stop them.'

'I've called the meeting of all the
wizards and dragons and anyone else who
wants to attend, at the standing stones at
midnight. First, we need to make sure
that we are right and that it is a rock
goblin or even more than one goblin,
causing all this trouble.

'And once we have confirmed our
suspicions, we need to come up with a
plan to stop them eating everything
before there is nothing left to eat except
Macdonald's.'

'Perhaps they could do a burger big enough to feed a goblin?' Grey suggested.

'I don't think they could make them fast enough to feed a rock goblin let alone more than one,' Red said, shaking her head. 'I don't want to turn another rock goblin to stone unless we really have to. Maybe we could convince them to go back to their hole in the ground.'

'And how do you propose we can do that?'

'What is the one thing a rock goblin cannot resist?'

'Cheese,' Grey said.

'Cheese indeed. Gorgonzola, to be precise. The strongest, smelliest, and yummiest cheese of all.'

'I know rock goblins have a penchant for cheese, but I didn't know Gorgonzola was their favourite,' Grey said. 'You learn something every day.'

'We could use some to draw them into the open and if we can get our claws on enough, keep them feasting until the sun comes up and then...' Red said, shaking her head. 'We would need to summon as much dragon magic as possible.'

'That is a good plan,' Grey said, agreeing.

'It's just an idea but it might work. Are any of your farms still producing cheese?'

'There are some further down the valley towards Ffestiniog, which had stock of milk and whey. They make blue cheese, and they might make Gorgonzola. How much do you think we'll need?'

'All of it,' Red said.

CHAPTER 5

At midnight that night, the dragons and wizards made their way to the standing stones using their cloaking devices and spells to hide from the humans. It was a sight to be seen with so many magicians and dragons of every colour gathered together.

White witches stood with dark witches and elves mingled with nymphs. There was chattering among the crowd. Some of them hadn't seen each other for a

hundred years or more and the

atmosphere was tense and exciting. Old

Red looked around at the attendees and

decided that everyone who needed to be

there was there.

Next to her, at her shoulder, was Old

Grey. The two huge dragons held court

and signalled for quiet. Within seconds,

silence had fallen across the meeting.

'You all know why you have been

summoned to this meeting,' said Red.

'There is mischief afoot on the island and

in the mountains beyond. You all know

what has been happening to the livestock,

and the only reasonable explanation is

that we have a rock goblin on the loose.'

'But all the rock goblins were turned

to stone many years ago,' the wizard from

Betws-y-coed said.

'All the rock goblins that we knew

about were turned to stone, but there is a

new outbreak,' Red said. 'We think that

the humans have dug too deep in the gold

mines and opened a chasm between us

and their domain.' Black smoke billowed

from her nostrils and her eyes glowed

yellow in the darkness. She was a

fearsome dragon when holding a meeting.

'We also think that the scale of the

mischief is such, that the only explanation

is that there is more than one goblin on

the rampage.'

'Oh no!'

'More than one?'

'That can't be!'

Uneasy chatter spread among the

gathering. Voices were raised and

questions were asked out of turn. Not

everyone agreed with the explanation and

even the ones that did were shocked and

stunned at the possibility that rock

goblins had been released from beneath

the mountains.

'How can you be sure it's a rock

goblin?'

'Do you have any proof?'

'This is all speculation!'

'Be quiet, everyone,' a voice boomed

from the back of the crowd. The crowd

parted to see who was speaking. It was

the ogre who lived beneath the Miners

Bridge at Betws-y-coed.

Ogres come in many shapes and

forms, but this one was huge. Twice the

size of a bear and three times as strong.

He went by the name of Mole, and he

could often be heard wondering through

the forests near Betws, singing and

chuckling to himself, *I am a mole and I live in a hole.*

The song amused him greatly, as he was called Mole, and he did indeed live in a hole.

'I, for one, think the dragons are right this time, which is a first for me. You all know I'm not a huge fan of these overgrown crocodiles, but they are absolutely correct in their assumptions.'

'Overgrown crocodiles?'

'Cheeky ogre!'

'This ogre has no respect for anyone. Why are we even listening to him?' someone shouted.

'Mole and his family have been keeping the rivers and lakes of our land crystal clear and clean for centuries,' Red said, shaking her head and smiling. 'And he also has a cheeky sense of humour. He's been calling me a crocodile since he was a young ogre. So, let him speak!' Old Red growled. The crowd fell quiet. 'Speak, Mole, my friend.'

'You will listen to me if you have any sense,' Mole said. 'I'm here because I have information for you which will confirm what Old Red is saying.' The gathering settled down and quiet fell. 'I have been following footsteps around the

Swallow Falls and they are footsteps such as I haven't seen for a very long time.'

'There are dragons near the falls,' a wizard argued.

'These footsteps are bigger than any dragons and they have eight toes.' A murmur spread through the crowd. The ogre nodded and grinned. His teeth were crooked and the size of plates. 'We all know that the only creature with feet so big and eight toes is a rock goblin. Judging by the size of the tracks they're leaving, they're fully grown adult rock goblins and there are indeed two of them.'

'What are they doing at Swallow Falls?'
a voice shouted.

'What rock goblins do best,' Mole replied. 'Eating. I checked the rivers that run through the town and there were no fish to be seen beyond the Swallow Falls. Fish do not just disappear, nor do they swim upstream in the winter, which means just one thing, something is eating them.'

'There we have it. We have all the evidence we need to establish that we have not one but two rock goblins on the loose,' Red said. 'And they're travelling from Betws through the mountains to

Anglesey, devouring everything they can on the way. Does everybody agree?'

A resounding yes rippled through the crowd. Everyone agreed that it was rock goblins to blame.

'What are we going to do about it?' one of the yellow dragons asked.

'We already have a plan,' Red said. 'We're going to lure the rock goblins out into the open.'

'And how on earth are you going to do that?'

'Gorgonzola cheese,' Red said, orange flames flew from her nostrils. 'We're going to gather as much stinky cheese as we possibly can and put it somewhere

that the goblins have to pass by.' Red

looked around the gathering. 'Two adult

rock goblins are powerful foes with

awesome speed and strength. The only

way for us to defeat them is to draw them

into the open and keep them there until

the sunrise.' The crowd nodded in

agreement. 'The sunlight will weaken

them enough for us to work our magic. It

will be dangerous for all involved, but if

we leave these pesky goblins, they will eat

and grow to be so strong, nothing will be

able to stop them.'

'If the goblins are eating the fish at Swallow Falls and then going to Anglesey to steal from the farmers, they will have to go along the Ogwen Valley.' Mole the ogre chuckled to himself. 'If I was going to put Gorgonzola cheese out as a trap, I would put it somewhere high where the smell will waft all around. Nowhere could be better for that than Tryfan.'

Another murmur spread through the crowd, all the wizards and dragons agreeing with what the cheeky ogre had to say.

'Thank you, Mole,' Old Red said. 'Let me know when the fish have returned beneath the falls.'

'My pleasure,' Mole said. The ogre turned and walked away, singing his tune, I am a mole and I live in a hole, chuckling to himself as he went.

'The ogre is right,' Red said. 'We have our plan, and we know what we must do. We must enlist the help of the nocturnal creatures, owls, bats, and rodents to gather as much cheese as we possibly can and get it to the top of Tryfan before the sun comes up.'

'What do you want us wizards and

witches to do?'

'We need you to go to the stone circle

at Porth-y-felin parc and use it to focus all

your powers onto the top of Tryfan. We're

going to need all the help we can get.'

CONRAD JONES

The Ogre Mole from beneath the Miners' Bridge.

Chapter 6

The sky that night was blackened by the wings of a thousand bats, owls, and insects. They each carried a minute crumb of Gorgonzola to the top of Tryfan. Minute by minute, the cheese pile became a cheese mound, and the mound became a hill. There were only a few hours left before sunrise when the last piece of blue cheese was dropped onto the summit. Old Red and Big Grey looked at each other and inhaled deeply. They let out the most ear-piercing roars, anyone had ever heard.

Their voices carried across the

mountains and the sea, striking fear into

the hearts of everyone who heard them.

Red sprayed fire across the top of the

tons of cheese, toasting the top. The

smell was delicious and it carried on the

wind far and wide. And then they waited.

And they waited.

And they waited.

And they waited.

And they waited.

An hour went by when a flash of

movement was seen on the slate mine

near Bethesda. One flash, almost a blur,

followed by a second. The rock goblins moved so fast; it was impossible to see them with the human eye. Red could see them coming as they scurried on all fours like huge greyhounds chasing the hare.

'They're coming,' Red whispered.

'Take to the air!'

The dragons took off from the mountain in silence, their huge wings flapping in the wind as they glided upwards on the updrafts. Greys flew next to Greens and Yellows, the Blues next to Reds and Browns. All the dragons climbed high into the atmosphere with Old Red leading them. As the rock goblins reached Tryfan, the wizards and witches at the stone circle in Porth-y-felin Parc began their magical chanting. Their magic wands, staffs, and sticks were pointed skywards towards Snowdonia as they began to circle the stones. They walked quicker and quicker, their chanting becoming louder. The stone circle began to glow, each stone filled with the power and energy of the ancient people who placed them there. The glow became dazzling and then sparked and fizzled like a miniature lightning storm. Electricity arced across the stone circle and the smell of burning filled the air. The sorcerers chanted louder trying to be heard above the lightning but soon their voices were drowned out by the thunder they'd created, yet still they walked and still they chanted, channelling all their energy at Tryfan.

Red dipped one wing and flew in a huge circle around the mountain. The other dragons followed, picking up speed, their wings flapping, becoming a deafening roar as they accelerated. The greedy rock goblins dived into the toasted Gorgonzola and began to stuff their faces with the gooey cheese. Its strong flavour and irresistible stink overwhelmed them.

They were oblivious to the first beams of

sunlight appearing in the east.

The wizards and witches summoned

all the ancient magic they could muster

and aimed it at the mountains, draining

the energy from the rock goblins without

them realising. Red and the other dragons

circled the mountain top at a thousand

miles an hour and a ring of light so bright

it would blind you, engulfed Tryfan. The

power of the dragons was awesome. One

of the rock goblins felt the sun on her skin

but the sorcerers' spell held him. As the

sun rose, the goblins darted for cover, but

they couldn't avoid the blinding light of

the dragon force. Red roared with deafening power, like thunder and the rock goblins stood straight and tall, unable to move. The sunlight engulfed them, and the power of the dragons penetrated their very souls, turning them to stone where they stood.

CHAPTER 7

Of course, the rock goblins are still at the top of Tryfan and you can see them if you are on the Betws side of the mountain looking up at the top.

From a car, they look like two people standing on the summit, but closer inspection reveals they are huge. The humans call them Adam and Eve, but they were in fact, both female rock goblins. No harm will come to them while they stand there, and the dragons will take them back to their home beneath the

mountains when the time is right. Old Red

still lives under Holyhead Mountain, and

she will be there forever and a day,

looking out for the people of the island

and beyond. Little Blue still climbs the

Tinto chimney or sometimes the mast at

RAF Valley. The other rock goblins will be

where they are now for a thousand years

or so and pose no harm to humans. They

don't hurt anyone, they're just greedy but

their greed makes so many others

unhappy and poor.

The dragons learnt a lesson this time

that no matter what colour their scales

were, they are all dragons and together

they could overcome evil.

The stone circle on Porth-y-felin is still

there in the park as are the standing

stones at Ty Mawr. If you haven't seen

them, you've never felt the magic they

possess. The magic within them is within

us all, you just have to find it. It's called

kindness and just like the wizards and

witches, if you point your kindness in the

right direction, wonderful things can

happen.

And remember, the dragons are

keeping an eye on things.

The Rock Goblins on Tryfan.

Printed in Great Britain
by Amazon

24094493R00061